*To Molly*

Rabén and Sjögren Bokförlag, Stockholm
www.raben.se
Translation copyright © 2001 by Rabén and Sjögren Bokförlag
All rights reserved
Originally published in Sweden by Eriksson & Lindgren under the title *Kottens hemlighet*
Text and pictures copyright © 2000 by Lena Anderson
Library of Congress catalog card number 2001 130145
Printed in Italy
First American edition, 2001
ISBN 91-29-65389-4

# LENA ANDERSON

# Hedgehog's Secret

Translated by *Elisabeth Kallick Dyssegaard*

## R&S
BOOKS

Stockholm New York London Adelaide Toronto

In the summer evening, stars are blinking.
Hedgehog strolls around while thinking.
She has a very secret treasure
that all night gives her so much pleasure.
While others are all sleeping tight,
Hedgehog's house is full of light.
Before too long she'll go to sleep
and into her dreams her treasure will creep.
What is her treasure? What could it be?
No one knows. It's not easy to see.

Through the curtains peeks the sun.
Wake up, Hedgehog, there's work to be done.
What a beautiful day for doing the wash.
The water sloshes, splish — splosh.
Hedgehog scrubs her clothes with care
and hangs them out to dry in the air.

Soon Hedgehog's friend stops by, too.
"I'm hungry," he says. "How about you?
Do you have anything that's good to eat,
like pizza, or pasta, or a special treat?
I really love peanut butter and jelly.
Can you hear the rumbling in my belly?"

"I really don't have time just now,
I hope you'll understand somehow.
We'll eat and play another day,
but now I have to go, okay?"
Hedgehog puts gooseberries in a pot
and cooks them till they're nice and hot.

Someone else comes to Hedgehog's place
with a lump in his throat and a tear on his face.
Sad little Teddy wants a hug from a friend,
and Hedgehog can always help in the end.
"Where's Hedgehog?" asks Teddy, with a very sad look.
Pig says, "Oh! Hedgehog could read you a book."

"I just don't have time for reading today,"
Hedgehog tells Teddy, "I'm sorry to say."
Hedgehog has a secret she doesn't want to tell.
She cooks and cleans and sweeps as well.
But she can't help her friends, or take time to play.
What is her secret? No one can say.

"What are you waiting for, you two?
You both look so gloomy, you really do,"
said Elephant as she walked in the door
while Hedgehog was busy cleaning the floor.
"Why don't we all of us go for a walk?
We could get some fresh air, and have time to talk."
"Oh no," said Hedgehog. "I've no time for that stuff."
So Elephant starts to leave in a huff.

"Don't be sad," Hedgehog said,
"you're still my good friend,
but today I have so many things to mend."

Elephant left, and outside met Pig.
"Something's up," she said, "and it's something big.
She's cleaning all over and making such a fuss,
she must know something she's not telling us."

Here comes Lottie — "Let's do something fun.
It's so warm and nice out here in the sun.
Let's go for a swim down by the lake;
a towel and a swimsuit is all we need take.
And we could go fishing, and see what we catch.
If we get any fish, we'll fry them up in a batch."

"No, I just don't have time, I'm sorry, I don't.
My house must be in order; if I don't clean it, it won't.
You'll just have to wait, all four of you."
But waiting is something that's no fun to do.
Hedgehog comes out at last, and swings her arms wide.
"I'm finally ready," she says with great pride.
"Now I can show you what I have inside . . ."

"My secret is just too wonderful to hide."

Later they eat all of the gooseberry stew
while baby Hedgehog sucks her thumb, too.
She is so little she barely makes a sound.
She lies very still and looks all around.

After a while, more and more guests stop by.
They've all heard the news and want to say hi.
The stars in the pale summer night start to shine,
and Hedgehog sits thinking, Isn't this fine?
I have so many friends, and friends make you rich.
Then her heart fills with music in perfect pitch.
"Shall we dance, little Hedgehog, just you and me?
Welcome to the world. It's a great place to be."

"Good night, my treasure."